Sci-Fi Spy Guy

Contents

Chapter 1	**A Wake up Call**	Page 5
Chapter 2	**I Spy**	Page 9
Chapter 3	**Spaced Out**	Page 14
Chapter 4	**Show Time**	Page 18
Chapter 5	**Down to Earth**	Page 23
Science Fiction		Page 30
Questions		Page 32

Badger Publishing

Vocabulary:

Alien - a person from another, very different place

Celebrity - a famous person

Limo - a large car

Planet - a large round object that orbits a star

Main Characters:

Jack - the star of a top rated children's TV show

Zarg - an extra terrestrial fan

STEALTH (Space Tripping Extra Atomic Laser Time Hopper)

Sci-Fi Spy Guy

by Roger Hurn

Illustrated by
Anthony Williams

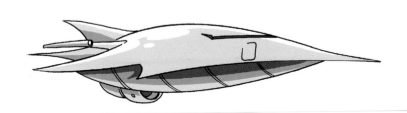

FULL FLIGHT

Titles in Full Flight 7

Midsummer Mutants	David Orme
Beekeeper	Danny Pearson
Labyrinth	Melanie Joyce
The Incredible Save	Alison Hawes
Sci-Fi Spy Guy	Roger Hurn
Ghost Camp	Jillian Powell
Stone Beasts	Richard Taylor
Alien Speed Smash	Jonny Zucker
Jet Pack Power	Jonny Zucker
Hero: A War Dog's Tale	Jane A C West

Badger Publishing Limited
Suite G08, Business & Technology Centre
Bessemer Drive, Stevenage, Hertfordshire SG1 2DX
Telephone: 01438 791037   Fax: 01438 791036
www.badger-publishing.co.uk

Sci-Fi Spy Guy ISBN 978-1-84926-257-6

Text © Roger Hurn 2010
Complete work © Badger Publishing Limited 2010

Badger Publishing would like to thank Jonny Zucker
for his help in putting this series together.

Publisher: David Jamieson
Editor: Danny Pearson
Design: Fiona Grant
Illustration: Anthony Williams
Printed and bound in China through Colorcraft Ltd., Hong Kong

Chapter 1
A Wake Up Call

Jack's doorbell rang.

The limo had arrived to take him to the
TV studios.

Jack was the star of the hit show Sci-Fi
Spy Guy.

He stumbled out of bed and flung his
clothes on.

He must have overslept.

He wondered why his Mum hadn't
woken him.
He guessed she must have overslept too.

Well I can soon fix that, he thought as
he dashed out of the front door and
slammed it behind him with a loud
crash.

Jack dived into the limo.

The driver had his cap pulled down low.

Jack couldn't see the man's face but Jack knew it wasn't his usual driver.

"Where's Billy today?" he said.

The man mumbled something.
Jack shrugged.

He didn't really care who drove him to the studio. All he wanted to do was go back to sleep.

He settled back down into his soft leather seat and was soon dozing happily.

He didn't see the driver glance back at him.

If he had, Jack would have been shocked to see that the driver's eyes glowed red in the dark!

Chapter 2
I Spy

Something was wrong.

Jack looked around the deserted TV studio. Where was everybody?

He glanced up at the studio clock and groaned.

It was four o'clock in the morning! Jack wasn't supposed to be on set until 7 am.

No wonder he was still half asleep.

That new limo driver got the wrong pick up time, thought Jack.

Now I've got to hang around for ages waiting for everyone to turn up.

Jack wandered round the set.

He stared at STEALTH - the Space Tripping Extra Atomic Laser Time Hopper.

This was the craft he used each week in his battle to save the universe from evil.

It sat there like a sleek, shiny steel dart just waiting to blast off into space.

Jack smiled. "I know you're not a real star ship," he said to STEALTH, "but you really do look the business."

Then, to his surprise, STEALTH's engines began to hum.

"No way!" gasped Jack. "This can't be happening. You don't have engines - you have sound effects. You're just a model."

Then an idea hit Jack. Every week he played the role of a Sci-Fi Spy on TV but now he had a real life Sci-Fi mystery to solve. "Come on Spy Guy," he said. "Let's do it."

Jack pulled open the door of the craft and scrambled inside.

To his amazement the driver of the limo was sitting at STEALTH's control desk.

He grinned at Jack and his eyes glowed red.

Then he hit the ignition.

"Hold on tight, Jack," he said.

"This may be a bumpy ride."

Chapter 3
Spaced Out

"Who the hell are you?" said Jack. "And just what is going on here?"

The alien grinned at him. "My name is Zarg," he said. "I'm from the Planet Zargon and I'm your biggest fan."

Jack's mouth fell open and he shook his head in disbelief. Then he fell over backwards as STEALTH shuddered, shook and then blasted off straight towards the studio ceiling.

"You maniac," yelled Jack. "You'll kill us both!"

"Don't panic," said Zarg cheerfully. "I've got it all under control."

The alien flipped a switch on the display screen and the onrushing ceiling disappeared to be replaced by the inky blackness of space.

Jack scrambled back up onto his feet and stared at the screen in amazement.

Then a large red planet came into view.

"That's Zargon," said Zarg. "You're going to love it there, Jack. You're going to be the star guest of the Sci-Fi Spy Guy Fan Club."

"What are you talking about?" said Jack.

He couldn't believe what he was hearing.
"And how come STEALTH is in space - it's only a model."

The alien chuckled. It sounded like water gurgling down a drain.

"I replaced your **S**pace **T**ripping **E**xtra **A**tomic **L**aser **T**ime **H**opper with the real thing when I came to Earth. I put the model in the studio car park under a large sheet."

Before Jack could reply, Zarg pushed a button on the control pad.

STEALTH rocketed down at warp speed to land on the planet.

But Jack smashed down hard onto the deck - again!

Chapter 4
Show Time

Jack stepped out of STEALTH to be greeted by a mob of fans.

They chanted his name and held up banners saying

"WELCOME TO ZARGON SPY GUY!"

"Wave to them, Jack", said Zarg.
"You're their hero."

Jack waved half heartedly.
"But I'm only an actor in a TV show,"
he muttered.

"Yes, but Sci-Fi Spy Guy is the most
popular programme on Zargon TV,"
said Zarg. "We get it on our space
satellites. Everybody watches it."

"That's great," said Jack. "But I've got
to go back to Earth right now or I'm
going to be late for filming the next
episode."

"Oh you can't go home," said Zarg.

Jack looked at him. He couldn't help noticing that Zarg's eyes were glowing red again.

Suddenly, Jack had a really bad feeling about all of this.
"Why not?" he said.

"Because we, the Sci-Fi Spy Guy Fan Club, have a lovely cage all ready and waiting for you at the Alien Celebrity Zoo," replied Zarg.

Jack gulped. "But I'm not an alien," he said.

"You are to us," said Zarg. "And you're definitely a celebrity.

So you'll be the star attraction at the zoo. People will come from all over the planet just to see you. Now won't that be nice?"

Down to Earth

Jack was only an actor, but he hadn't spent the past two years playing the part of a dare devil, alien battling Sci-Fi spy for nothing.

He grabbed a banner from a nearby fan and whacked Zarg firmly on the head with it.

"Sorry about that, Zarg," he said.
"But I thought you'd like to see some
more stars!"

The alien crowd all cheered. "It's just
like watching Jack in Sci-Fi Spy Guy,"
they said to each other.
"Only this time it's for real!"

Zarg's eyes crossed and changed from red to amber to green like a traffic light.

"I guess that's green for go," said Jack as he dived back into STEALTH.

The door slid shut behind him.

He hurled himself over to the control desk and he hit the take off button.

STEALTH shook itself like a wet dog then hurtled up into the sky.

Soon Zargon was just a red dot in the depths of space.

"Well, so far so good," said Jack to himself. "But how do I pilot this thing home?"

He scratched his head.

Jack didn't like the idea of being stuck in space any better than the idea of being kept in a cage in the zoo.

Then he had an idea.

In the TV show his adventures always ended in the same way.

Jack shrugged. It's got to be worth a
try, he thought.

He cleared his throat and said in his
best Sci-Fi Spy Guy voice, "Take me
home, STEALTHY."

For a second nothing happened but
then STEALTH's computer said,
"HOME IT IS SPY GUY."

The engines hit warp speed, and the next thing Jack knew he was back in the studio sitting inside an alien space craft.

He glanced up at the display screen and saw the rest of the cast and crew staring at the star ship in amazement.

Then the director marched up to the
ship and banged on the door.

"Stop messing about, Jack," he yelled.
"We've got a TV show to film!"

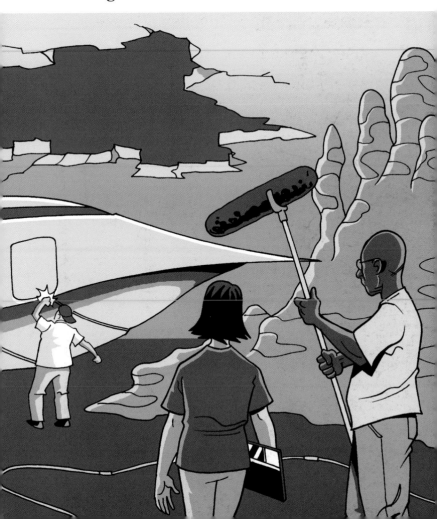

Science Fiction

Stories like Sci-Fi Spy Guy are called Science Fiction stories.

This is because they are often set in outer space and have aliens as major characters in the plot.

Science Fiction stories often feature very advanced technology such as time machines or star ships that can travel faster than the speed of light.

The first people to write science fiction books were a Frenchman called Jules Verne and an Englishman called H.G.Wells.

They are known as the "Fathers of science fiction".

They wrote their books over one hundred years ago but people still love to read them today.

Science Fiction is a very popular subject for TV shows, computer games and movies as well as for books.

The most popular science fiction films of all time are the Star Wars movies.

Doctor Who is the most popular science fiction show on UK television. It features a time travelling Time Lord called The Doctor.

He travels through time and space in a machine called the Tardis.

Questions

- Why didn't Jack care who drove him to the studio?

- What do the letters S.T.E.A.L.T.H. stand for?

- Where did Zarg take Jack?

- Where did the Zargons want to keep Jack?

- Was Jack happy to meet his fans on Zargon?

- Who were "The Fathers of Science Fiction"?

- What makes a story a science fiction story?

- What is the most popular science fiction show on British television?